Ready, Set, Go!

Read more

MOBY SHINOBI AND TOBY TOO!

books!

Surf's Up!

Take a Hike!

BUILDING

Ready, Set, Go!

Luke
Flowers

SCHOLASTIC INC.

To Rob McClurkan—thanks for helping me navigate the roads of this children's book creating adventure from the very start! You continue to provide the fuel of inspiration with your encouragement, creativity, and cherished friendship.

Library of Congress Cataloging-in-Publication Data

Names: Flowers, Luke, author, illustrator. | Flowers, Luke. Moby Shinobi and Toby too! ; 3.
Title: Ready, set, go! / Luke Flowers.
Description: First edition. | New York : Scholastic Inc., 2021. | Series: Moby Shinobi and Toby too! ; 3 | Summary: Told in rhyme, Moby Shinobi and his dog Toby volunteer to drive when his friend Jenny's junior race car driver fails to show up, but as usual his enthusiasm ends up in a mess of oil spills, flat tires, and wrong turns–but he redeems himself by repairing the oil leak, and wins the race for Jenny.
Identifiers: LCCN 2019059423 | ISBN 9781338547580 (library binding) | ISBN 9781338547573 (paperback) | ISBN 9781338604986 (ebk) Subjects: LCSH: Ninja–Juvenile fiction. | Helping behavior–Juvenile fiction. | Automobile racing–Juvenile fiction. | Stories in rhyme. | Humorous stories. | CYAC: Stories in rhyme. | Ninja–Fiction. | Helpfulness–Fiction. | Automobile racing–Fiction. | LCGFT: Stories in rhyme. | Humorous fiction.
Classification: LCC PZ8.3.F672 Re 2020 | DDC (E)–dc23
LC record available at https://lccn.loc.gov/2019059423

10 9 8 7 6 5 4 3 2 1   21 22 23 24 25

Printed in China   62
First edition, July 2021
Edited by Rachel Matson
Book design by Christian Zelaya

Table of Contents

On the Go

1

Toby wants to go super fast.
A racing day would be a blast!

3

Hats, camera, and megaphone.
Flag, water, and your squeaky bone!

Bo staff, nunchucks, and throwing stars.
Comic books about racing cars!

Speedy ninjas zip down the street.
Shinobi Go! We can't be beat!

Let's train on the way to the race.
We can start with a ninja chase!

7

Through the tunnel, out of the dark.
They zoom past players in the park!

STOP! Ninjas flip to the red light.

GO! They zip through cones, left and right.

9

Moby and Toby join the crowd!
Excited fans, all cheering loud!

Start Your Engines

Junior racers prepare their cars.
They all dream of being **big** stars!

14

Moby thinks of a quick trick throw!

The other cars will be so **slow**.

15

Your tank is cracked and leaking gas!
I think our chance to win will pass.

21

Snack Attack!

We need some snacks for the big race. The Track Shack is the perfect place.

24

BIG RACE
STARTS IN
88 minutes

THE TRACKSHACK

MENU

FIRE

WAY

The line just continues to grow.
WHEW! How much faster can we go?

Moby thinks of his ninja speed.

The fans will get the snacks they need!

29

FLIP!

SPIN!

34

You pull the cart, I'll toss each snack!

We will quickly finish this stack!

Every fan gets their snack in time!
DING-DONG! There goes the race bell chime!

Help! My whole team is feeling slow. My broken engine will not go!

41

With these tools, I know what to do!
Combine them all—make something new!

NUNCHUCKS

THROWING
STARS

ROAD
TAR

WRENCH

ZIP!

THUG BUG

NINJA ★ SPIN

GO! NINJA GO! #1

CHEER!

NINJA SPIN

Tires changed with a speedy twist!

Gas and oil checked off the list!

Moby's speed keeps them in first place!
Driver Dan zips back to the race!

One last lap left! Go, Ninja Spin!
Driver Dan zooms in for the **win**!

About the Author

Luke Flowers lives in Colorado Springs with his wife and three children. He learned to drive go-carts and dirt bikes on the farm where he grew up, and raced with his brothers! Thankfully they never had  any big crashes … but they DID have some BIG fun together.

Luke has illustrated over sixty books, including *New York Times* bestseller *A Beautiful Day in the Neighborhood* by Fred Rogers and *Unicorn Day* by Diana Murray. But being able to write AND illustrate the Moby Shinobi series has been the most HI-YAH-wesome highlight of his creative journey.

YOU CAN DRAW A RACE CAR!

1 Draw the outline of your car.

2 Draw the wheels, the bumpers, and the windshield.

3 Add your driver.

4 Color in your drawing!

WHAT'S YOUR STORY?

Moby and Toby help fix Driver Dan's race car.
Imagine that **you** are racing too!
What would your car look like?
How would you give it super speed?
Write and draw your story!

scholastic.com/acorn